merrygoround
15 Kirk Wynd
Kirkcaldy 4177

INSIDE

OUTSIDE

UPSIDE DOWN

INSIDE

OUTSIDE

UPSIDE DOWN

by Stan and Jan Berenstain

A Beginning Beginner Book
COLLINS AND HARVILL

Trademark of Random House, Inc., William Collins Sons & Co. Ltd., Authorised User

ISBN 0 00 171204 7
COPYRIGHT © 1968 BY RANDOM HOUSE, INC.
A BRIGHT AND EARLY BOOK FOR BEGINNING BEGINNERS
PUBLISHED BY ARRANGEMENT WITH RANDOM HOUSE, INC.,
NEW YORK, NEW YORK
FIRST PUBLISHED IN GREAT BRITAIN 1969
PRINTED IN GREAT BRITAIN
COLLINS CLEAR-TYPE PRESS: LONDON AND GLASGOW

Going in

Inside

Inside a box

Upside down

Inside a box
Upside down

Going out

Outside

Outside
Inside a box
Upside down

Going on

On a truck
Outside
Inside a box
Upside down

Going

Going to town
On a truck
Outside
Inside a box
Upside down

Falling off

Off the truck

Coming out

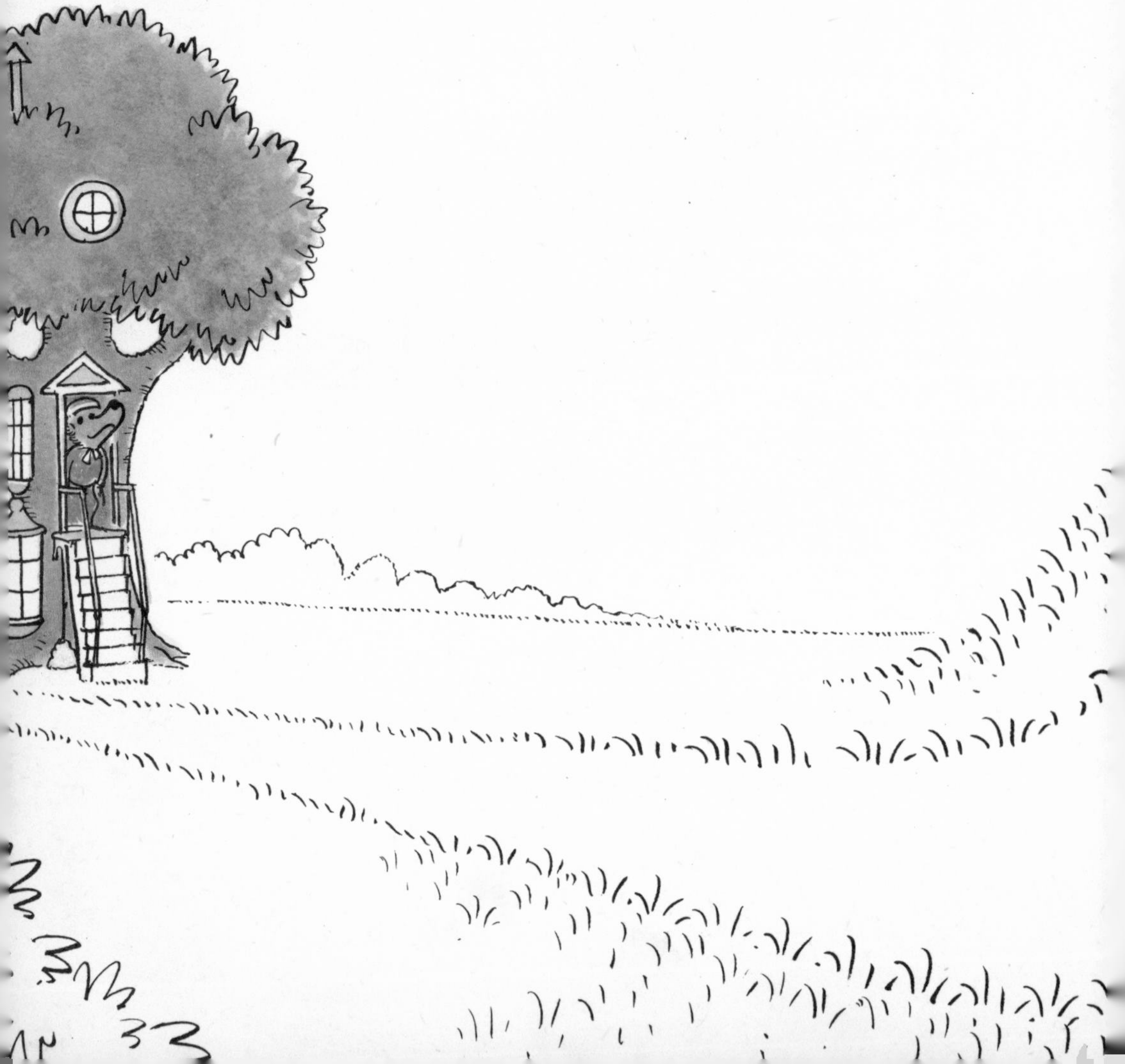

Right side up!

Mama! Mama!
I went to town.
Inside,
Outside,
Upside down!